W9-ABS-246

Take It from Me

Other books in the Young Women of Faith Library

The Lily Series
Here's Lily!
Lily Robbins, M.D. (Medical Dabbler)
Lily and the Creep
Lily's Ultimate Party
Ask Lily
Lily the Rebel
Lights, Action, Lily!
Lily Rules!

Non-Fiction
The Beauty Book
The Body Book
The Buddy Book
The Best Bash Book
The Blurry Rules Book
The It's MY Life Book
The Creativity Book
The Uniquely Me Book
Dear Diary
Girlz Want to Know
NIV Young Women of Faith Bible
YWOF Journal: Hey! This Is Me

Young Women of Faith

Take It from Me

straight talk about life from a teen who's been there

by Molly Buchan

Zonder**kidz**

Zonder**kidz**™

The children's group of Zondervan

www.zonderkidz.com

Take It from Me
Copyright © 2002 by Women of Faith

Requests for information should be addressed to:
Grand Rapids, Michigan 49530

ISBN: 0–310–70316–6

All Scripture quotations, unless otherwise indicated, are taken from the HOLY
BIBLE, NEW INTERNATIONAL VERSION ®. Copyright © 1973, 1978, 1984
by International Bible Society. Used by permission of Zondervan. All rights
reserved.

Scripture marked NASB is taken from the NEW AMERICAN STANDARD
BIBLE ®. Copyright © 1960, 1962, 1963, 1968, 1971, 1972, 1973, 1975, 1977, 1995
by The Lockman Foundation. Used by permission.

All rights reserved. No part of this publication may be reproduced, stored in a
retrieval system, or transmitted in any form or by any means — electronic,
mechanical, photocopy, recording, or any other — except for brief quotations in
printed reviews, without the prior permission of the publisher.

Zonderkidz is a trademark of Zondervan.

Published in association with the literary agency of Alive Communications, Inc.,
7680 Goddard Street, Suite 200, Colorado Springs, CO 80920.

Editor: Barbara J. Scott
Cover Artwork: Elizabeth Brandt
Art direction: Michelle Lenger
Interior design: Susan Ambs

Printed in the United States of America

02 03 04 05/❖ DC/5 4 3 2 1

To my grandmother, Nan Buchan,
who always called me Princess
—even when I didn't act like one.

CONTENTS

Jump Start—What a Healthy Self-Image Looks Like   9

Top Secret—Somebody Loves You!   17

Enemy #1—The Copycat Caper   22

Enemy #2—The Skin-Deep Syndrome   29

Enemy #3—The Mannequin Mistake   38

Enemy #4—False Expectation Frustration   44

Enemy #5—The People-Pleasing Pit   50

Enemy #6—Victim Valley   58

Enemy #7—Failure Fixation   64

Enemy #8—Toxic Relationship Ruts   72

Enemy #9—Perfectionist Paralysis   79

Enemy #10—The Comfort-Zone Coffin   86

On Purpose—Finding Your Glass Slipper   92

Activation—Now Go Ahead and Shine!   100

Jump Start— What a Healthy Self-Image Looks Like

*Now we see but a poor reflection as in a mirror;
then we shall see face to face.*
—*1 Corinthians 13:12*

I'll never forget the day I went to the Ohio State Fair with my cousin Amy. One of our favorite stops was the House of Mirrors, where fat people look skinny and skinny people look fat, and *everyone* looks strange. Although we could recognize ourselves, it was clear that the mirrors weren't giving us an accurate picture of what we really looked like.

Some kids live in a House of Mirrors. They see themselves in the twisted reflections that bounce back from those around them.

They're not too fat . . . but they *see themselves* as too fat.

They're not too skinny . . . but they *see themselves* as too skinny.

They're not stupid . . . but they *see themselves* as stupid.

They're not a failure . . . but they *see themselves* as a failure.

They're not unloved . . . but they *see themselves* as unlovable.

It might be fun visiting the House of Mirrors at an amusement park or state fair, but it sure wouldn't be fun to live your life there. In this book, I want to share with you how you can escape from the House of Mirrors and defeat the ten deadly enemies of positive self-esteem.

What Is Self-Esteem?

Self-esteem is our opinion of our own personal worth, competence, and importance. That means how we think and feel about ourselves. Sometimes our self-image is based on facts about our personality or looks, but lots of times it has nothing to do with what's real. The "mirrors" we use to evaluate our worth sometimes twist the image like those in the House of Mirrors, distorting the picture of how we see ourselves.

Most of us struggle with a poor self-image at one time or another. We see ourselves as ugly when we're pretty, unlovable when we're loved, unsuccessful even though we have succeeded, useless when we're talented, and worthless though we have great value.

When we suffer with low self-esteem, it's easy to think we're the only ones who feel that way. It may seem like everyone around us has it all together, while we're the "ugly duckling," the loser no one wants to hang out with. But believe it or not, just about *everyone* feels this way sometimes.

So how do you know if you have healthy self-esteem? Girls with good self-images:

- Don't give up easily.
- Aren't afraid to fail.
- Find ways to keep going and learn from the effort.
- Are willing to take risks, confident that success will come in the end.
- Know what they want and aren't embarrassed to ask for it.
- Choose good relationships.
- Hang out with others without losing their own sense of who they are.

Have discovered the joy of helping others rather than being all wrapped up with themselves.

Does It Really Matter?

Do you see how important self-esteem is? It affects every area of your life! If you have a poor self-image, it can mess up your thoughts, your emotions, your actions, and even your values. It can make you feel like no one wants you, needs you, or loves you. You'll end up feeling sorry for yourself.

A poor self-image can cause you to have problems with other people too. It can make you jealous and possessive of your friends—and that will usually make them want to get away from you. But a good self-image will help you to be outgoing and encouraging toward others. And everyone likes that kind of person.

Your self-image also plays a major role in your ability to fulfill your dreams. A negative self-image can destroy your creativity and motivation, leaving you feeling useless and depressed. You'll find yourself unable to start new things because your inner voice will keep telling you that you always mess things up and nothing works out for you anyway.

Escaping the House of Mirrors!

Here's good news: Your self-image isn't something you're stuck with forever. You weren't born with a poor self-image, and if you have one now, you don't need to keep it. Countless people who are successful and happy today were once timid and self-destructive. Even a lot of actors were once shy and gawky.

I know a woman who was really skinny when she was growing up. She felt that she was ugly, especially when her classmates called her names like "bird legs." However, she grew up to be a beautiful, shapely woman. The "ugly duckling" became a beautiful swan. What you think is bad about your looks may not be so bad later.

One of the aerobics instructors at the YMCA near our house is a young woman named Mandy. Although Mandy is overweight—not at all a beauty queen—she is one of the most popular aerobics instructors. Why? Because she *likes herself*. Instead of pulling away from people, she reaches out. Mandy decided not to take her physical appearance so seriously. People like her because she likes herself and is fun to be around.

Oprah's Story

Much of her life, TV and movie star Oprah Winfrey has struggled with being overweight. Yet it's hard to find a person who has a more positive image of herself. This is even more amazing when you look at her difficult childhood.

Oprah was born in Kosciusko, Mississippi, to unmarried teenage parents. For the first six years of her life, she lived in poverty on her grandmother's farm. Then she started staying on and off with her mother in Milwaukee, where she was sexually abused by male relatives. At age fourteen, Oprah gave birth to a premature baby who didn't survive. She then went to live with her father and step-mother in Nashville, where she did much better.

At her new home in Nashville, Oprah focused on her schoolwork and did so well that she was even able to skip several grades. She earned a scholarship to Tennessee State University and, while still in school, landed a job as co-anchor of the evening news at WTF-TV. Eventually, she became the hostess of the nation's most popular TV talk show and is now the world's highest-paid entertainer.

Who would have thought someone with so many early hardships would be so successful? The key was that Oprah never doubted she would reach the top. "All my life I have known I was born to greatness," she has said. She wasn't about to let her self-worth be determined by the negative House of Mirrors where she grew up.

Facing the Truth about Yourself

Before you can be set free from the crazy view you have formed of yourself in the House of Mirrors, you must face the *truth* about who you really are. It may not be a fun experience to face your true self, but the truth will set you free to grow into the person God created you to be.

Author and minister A. W. Tozer lists seven things you can ask yourself in order to find out who you really are:

- **What do I want the most?**
- **What do I think about the most?**
- **How do I use my money?**
- **What do I do with my free time?**
- **What kind of people do I hang out with?**
- **Who and what do I admire the most?**
- **What kinds of things do I laugh at?**

When you ask yourself these questions, do you like the person you see in your mirror? Do you think the person you see is who you really are or an image created by what other people say about you? If you can't decide, find a trustworthy adult who can give you some help with this.

It's hard to see ourselves as we really are in a world that often tells us lies about ourselves. Throughout this book, I'll use many examples of people who are well known—some are Christian and some are not—but each person has a story that might be helpful to you. Ultimately, I've found that the Bible is a mirror that always tells me the truth about who I am (see James 1:23–25). Friends change, feelings change, even our bodies change, but the Bible is a solid rock that always remains the same.

There's Hope!

If you struggle with low self-esteem . . .
If your self-esteem just needs a checkup . . .
If you wonder if your life can ever change . . .
This book is for you!

TOP SECRET—
SOMEBODY LOVES YOU!

But God demonstrates his own love for us in this:
While we were still sinners, Christ died for us.
—Romans 5:8

I'm a fortunate person, and I know it. Many people show me love. I come from a loving family and have lots of friends. Many people tell me I'm pretty, and I get enough attention from guys. I've done okay in school and in my other activities. To other people, it must seem like I have everything I need for a healthy self-image.

But I've come to some conclusions that may shock you:

! **Even though I have a wonderful family, they can't be the main source of my self-esteem.**

! **Even though I'm thankful for my friends, they can't be the main source of my self-esteem.**

! Even though I've been called attractive and experienced success, that can't be the main source of my self-esteem.

! Sure, all of these things are great, but my self-image is still on shaky ground unless there's something more.

Confession

When I was growing up, my dad was a minister, so we went to church all the time. I didn't think much about it one way or another, but my family's faith could only take me so far. By the time I reached my preteen years, I was beginning to develop a double life. I still went to church with my parents, but my friends and I were also starting to experiment with cigarettes and alcohol. I also started getting interested in boys and sometimes allowed them to get more romantic with me than I should have.

Girls who lead a double life will eventually have to lie to cover up their activities. I became a pretty convincing liar. When my parents weren't around, I learned to cuss—and some of the words coming out of my mouth definitely wouldn't have been accepted in church.

There I was, a "good" church kid finding ways to sin in secret. Was this the best of both worlds? No way! When I was with my parents or in church, I felt guilty and ashamed of what I was doing behind their backs. But when I was with my friends, I couldn't have any "fun" either, because I felt too guilty and ashamed of what I was doing!

Instead of having the best of both worlds, I couldn't enjoy *either* world. I learned a hard lesson from all this: A girl who doesn't have a clear conscience won't have positive self-esteem either.

Decision Time

I managed to hide my double life for a few years, but I knew it couldn't go on for long. I couldn't have it both ways. I either needed to follow God or follow my friends.

The conflict between my two lifestyles was tearing me up inside. Sometimes I leaned one way, and sometimes the other. My parents knew I was having a hard time, but they didn't know how to help me. All they could do was love me—and watch and pray.

Even though I enjoyed partying with my friends, I really didn't like the person I became when I was around them. On the other hand, I noticed that when I was close to God, my family, and my Christian friends, I had more peace and felt better about myself.

One day I surrendered my life completely to God. "Lord," I prayed, "I'm tired of trying to run my own life. I need you to take full control and make me the kind of person you want me to be."

Sure, I still have struggles since I gave my life to the Lord. But now my life has more peace and direction than I've ever experienced before.

Finding the Love You Need

Imagine this scene: The greatest guy in the whole world is madly in love with you! He's rich, kind, handsome, and has a fantastic personality—everything you've ever wanted in a guy. You can hardly believe it. He could have had any girl he wanted, and he wants *you*!

This is not just a fairy tale. There is someone who loves you enough to have died for you. He is the greatest thing that could ever happen to your self-esteem, and you don't have to be concerned about him ever dumping you. Even when you're having a bad day, his love for you is as strong as ever.

I found this love in Jesus Christ, and you can too. He's the only solid rock you can build a strong self-image upon. Let him turn your self-image into a God-image! His love for you isn't based on the way you look, your good grades, or being perfect. He loves you the way you are, and he loves you enough to help you make necessary changes.

If you haven't yet discovered this amazing love of God, I encourage you to do so today. It's great to have the love of your family and friends, but this is a love that's far more incredible than anything you've ever known.

Somebody loves you! It's the love you've been looking for!

ENEMY #1—

THE COPYCAT CAPER

*Do not conform any longer to the pattern of this world,
but be transformed by the renewing of your mind.*
—Romans 12:2

Going to a new school is always a little scary—especially when it's middle school and you don't know anybody there yet. Often people already have their friends, and usually those friendships are hard to break into. The cliques have already formed, and if you aren't in the "in crowd" you will have to get used to being an outsider.

When I started a new middle school, I found that all the girls there wore lots of makeup. I figured I would fit in better if I wore more makeup too. I did everything I could to fit in with the styles of the popular girls, changing my makeup, hairstyle, and wardrobe.

But it didn't work! I felt totally miserable. I never did become part of the popular crowd, and trying to just created a *new* problem: I wasn't true to myself. Even though I was a pretty good copycat, deep inside I knew it wasn't the real me. It was just an act. I was trying to squeeze myself into a mold that would never fit.

The Bible warns us about this. It says, "Do not conform any longer to the pattern of this world, but be transformed by the renewing of your mind" (Romans 12:2). Instead of trying to pattern ourselves after the people around us, we are supposed to let God change our lives. He wants to change us into *his* image.

Not only have I *been* a copycat at times, but I have also had friends who tried to copy me. This can be flattering—up to a point. But then it would get annoying. You can't help wondering, *Why don't they get a life? Don't they have any opinions of their own?*

Once I had a friend named Christy (not her real name) who tried to copy everything I did. When I got my nails done, she had to get her nails done. When I got a new haircut, she got one just like mine. When I got my ears pierced, she rushed out to the mall to get hers pierced too. Soon she was dressing like me, talking like me, and laughing like me.

What's wrong with this picture? It's natural for close friends to be like each other in some ways, but it's also important that they each have a sense of their own identity. A person with a healthy self-image won't be a copycat. They will accept themselves enough to realize that getting a makeover every week won't make them popular.

Never pretend to be something you aren't! I realize that this can be difficult, because at this point you still might be trying to figure out who you really are. But remember this: If the people around you can't accept you for who you are, they definitely won't accept you if you try to act like somebody else.

You are unique and special. Don't settle for being a cheap copy of someone else. Even if you succeeded in copying another person, you would only be a copy. Don't forget that. Nothing can be better than who God created you to be!

The Comparison Trap

I've learned the hard way that a positive self-image will never come by comparing yourself to others. If you constantly compare yourself with someone who is beautiful, smart, and popular, you'll just get depressed. You'll feel as if you can never measure up to such a high standard, and your self-esteem will fall to zero.

On the other hand, perhaps you enjoy comparing yourself to those who are less attractive, less intelligent, and less popular than you. You may even think that such comparisons are a great boost to your self-esteem. *Well, at least I'm better than that loser!* you might think to yourself. But is that the way to gain healthy self-esteem? No, and here's why: Comparing yourself to those you think are inferior to you will just turn you into a proud, critical, and judgmental person. You've probably met kids like that, and they aren't much fun to be around.

You might ask, "Isn't there *anyone* I can compare myself to?" Yes, there is. You can compare yourself as you are today with the person you want to become someday. In other words, the person you need to compare yourself with is *you!* You need to be the best version of yourself that you can be. As author Neil Eskelin puts it, "You aren't in competition with anyone but yourself."

In case you aren't sure what kind of person you want to be, there's someone you should get to know. His name is Jesus! He's the perfect model of what God wants each of us to be like. We should become more like him every day.

Do You Feel Like a "Second Fiddle"?

Some kids struggle with self-esteem because they're comparing themselves with a talented friend or brother or sister who always seems to be more successful. The key is not to compete with them, but to find your own place in life. Instead of feeling bad about yourself because of the accomplishments of someone else, you need to discover your own gifts. You will only hurt yourself if you try to hinder the success of others, but your self-image will improve if you become an encourager to those around you.

Leonard Bernstein, a famous orchestra conductor, was once asked what was the hardest instrument to play. He replied without hesitation, "Second fiddle! I can always get plenty of first violinists, but to find one who plays second violin with as much enthusiasm or second French horn or second flute, now that's a problem. And yet if no one is willing to play second, we have no harmony."

You will find much more harmony and happiness in your life if you're willing to play "second fiddle" at times, supporting others in their leading role. Instead of being a copycat or trying to tear down others who seem more successful than you are, use your energy to find your own special place of service and achievement.

Poet T. S. Eliot once warned, "Most of the trouble in the world is caused by people wanting to be important." Eliot's remark could be restated this way: Most of the trouble in the world is caused by people who have low self-esteem and are competing with others for popularity and success.

In her book *40 Days with God*, Rebecca St. James shares the key to true happiness: "We don't need 'stuff' to be happy—the perfect body, or the best-looking car, the most up-to-date clothes, or the best house on the best street. We need Jesus Christ to be our total priority and not let that other stuff get in the way. I think this is the key to happiness."

The Hollywood Charade

Many girls today are obsessed with the latest teen magazines, models, musicians, and movie stars. They hang pictures of these beautiful celebrities on their walls and wish that they could somehow look more like them. "Wow! Look at that complexion!" they say. "She has such a perfect face—no zits at all! And what I wouldn't give to have a body like that!"

How can you compete with the stars of Hollywood or Nashville? The answer is simple—you can't! The more you try to compare yourself with these celebrities, the more your self-esteem will come crashing down. Even they get depressed when they compare themselves with each other!

Yes, there are some very attractive people on the covers of the magazines you can't help but notice at the grocery store checkout counters. But you also need to realize a very important secret about these stars: In real life, they hardly ever can live up to the image they portray on the magazine covers or in music videos and movies.

If you saw your favorite stars up close, you might be amazed to see that they have pimples and blemishes too. But the pictures on the magazine covers are the product of hours of photo shoots and the "technological computer magic" needed to retouch the pictures and remove every facial imperfection. The result? The images projected are definitely better than how the stars really look. What you see is not what they look like in real life. If you compare yourself to these Hollywood charades, your self-esteem will always struggle.

Be yourself. Nobody likes a copycat.

Enemy #2—

The Skin-Deep Syndrome

Man looks at the outward appearance,
but the Lord looks at the heart.
—1 Samuel 16:7

You might think that beauty and a positive self-image always go hand in hand, but that's not necessarily the case. Let me tell you the surprising stories of two girls I've known.

A beautiful girl named Nicki was in my dance class several years ago. She was a nice girl, but I got really irritated when she wouldn't stop looking at herself on the mirrored walls of the dance studio, even when the instructor was talking to us. She would nervously tinker with her hair and look at herself from different angles to make sure she wasn't getting fat. During the breaks, Nicki would often ask the other girls whether they thought she looked good in the outfit she had on. Although she was clearly one of the prettiest girls in the class, she would frequently make negative comments about herself: "Don't you think my nose is too big?" or "Would my hair look better a lighter color?" or "I wish I had pretty eyes like yours."

I have another friend who's quite different from Nicki. Robin's short and a little overweight, but that doesn't seem to bother her. She would never win a beauty contest. Yet Robin is always a blast to be around. She doesn't compare herself to others, and she's comfortable with who she is. Because she has a good self-image, people love being with Robin.

Instead of being stuck on herself like Nicki, Robin reaches out to others and makes them feel good about themselves. She's invited to all the parties because everyone knows she isn't competing with anyone for popularity. Her sense of humor brightens any occasion.

Do you see why people would be more attracted to Robin than to Nicki? By being so stuck on herself, Nicki became a hard person for others to love.

Many kids think, *I would feel great about myself if I looked like that person.* But would they really? Positive self-esteem is mostly a decision to think well of ourselves, no matter how outwardly attractive we may be. Have you made that decision? Or are you wasting your time feeling sorry for yourself and thinking about all the things you don't like about yourself—things you probably have no way of changing?

Jessica's Struggle

If you sometimes dislike your looks, you're not alone. Take the example of pop-singer Jessica Simpson. Now I'm not trying to set her up as a role model for you to follow. I just want you to realize that even someone as physically beautiful as she is has battled with the same feelings. For many years she has struggled with low self-esteem, worrying about her weight and never feeling thin enough.

Sometimes other people say things that are very damaging to our self-image. At one of Jessica Simpson's first photo shoots for a national magazine, a photographer told her she had fat arms. Jessica left the studio in tears. "There are many people who seem really confident but who have low self-esteem internally," Jessica explains. "It can be something you don't like about yourself: *'Oh, I'm not smart enough.'* For me it has always been a physical thing."

If you base your worth on your physical appearance, you will never be happy. Jessica's high school journals are filled with references to her inner battle. When she was seventeen, Jessica wrote:

Why did you eat that? You're never going to look good! What will people think? Your face is so broken out. You're fat! Another Coke?! Eat, eat, eat, eat—don't you ever feel sick? I'm beginning to hate myself. What's wrong with me? Lately I've been forgetting the inside stuff and only concentrating on the outside.

Have you ever felt that way? I have! Once the head of a modeling agency told me I needed to lose some weight to be successful. That was really hard on me! For a while I tried starving myself with all kinds of crazy diets, and I was even tempted to become anorexic or bulimic. When I was challenged by my parents and Christian friends, God helped me snap out of my foolish obsession with my outward appearance.

Going Beyond the Surface

Many people project a beauty that is only skin-deep. They spend hours putting on their makeup, fixing their hair in the latest style, tanning their skin, and working out in the gym. There's nothing wrong with any of this, as long as we remember that *true beauty must go below the surface.*

Can you imagine what we would be like if we spent as much time working on our inner beauty as we did on our outer beauty? What would our lives be like if we committed ourselves to developing a sincere concern for others, patience when wronged, and joy even when we're having a bad day? What kind of people would we be if our lives were marked by generosity instead of selfishness, a positive outlook instead of constant complaining?

Not long ago, I went with the youth group of my church to visit people in a nearby nursing home. I learned a big lesson that day. I'm not sure whether any of the people we visited had been beauty queens in their younger days. Even if they had once been dazzling beauties, most of them now looked pretty much the same.

However, the elderly people we saw that day showed a big contrast in their amount of *inner* beauty. Some were angry, bitter, and constantly grumbling about their lives. Even though we tried to reach out to them in love, their negative outlook prevented them from receiving it.

Other residents of the nursing home had a different attitude. Although they were old, weak, and wrinkled, they still had a cheery personality. When they spoke of their lives, they told delightful stories and shared pearls of wisdom that they had learned. These elderly saints had long ago lost their outward beauty, but their inner beauty was still going strong. We had come to the nursing home to brighten the day of the elderly residents, but these inwardly beautiful people brightened *our* day instead.

When you get old, which kind of person will you be? You might not want to face it, but your outward beauty won't last forever. As you get older, the issue of your inner beauty—or lack of it—will take center stage. The Bible gives a good promise, and warning, about this very thing: "Though outwardly we are wasting away, yet inwardly we are being renewed day by day" (2 Corinthians 4:16). If we are truly following Jesus, each day he will make us more beautiful on the inside.

Learning from Joni

Whenever I start getting snared by the skin-deep syndrome, I remember the story of Joni Eareckson Tada. Joni was an attractive, energetic, and popular teen when she was injured while diving in 1967. The accident left her paralyzed from her neck down. Although she was unable to use her hands during two difficult years of rehabilitation, she learned how to paint with a brush between her teeth. While her friends enjoyed the normal activities of their teen years, Joni struggled to adjust to her new life.

It would have been easy for Joni to let herself be trapped in a prison of self-pity and depression. But she didn't. In fact, she may well have accomplished more as a quadriplegic than she ever would have as a "normal" person. She has become famous all over the world as the author of twenty-seven books, a popular conference speaker, and even the subject of a movie about her life. She is the founder and president of Joni and Friends, a Christian ministry to the disabled. She is comforting others with the comfort she has received from God (2 Corinthians 1:5–6).

Do you see the amazing lesson we can learn from Joni about healthy self-esteem? If it depended on physical ability, Joni wouldn't stand a chance. But she has risen above her outward limitations, finding a fulfilling life by serving others in need. She radiates an inner beauty far beyond most "normal" people—a joy that comes from her relationship with Christ.

Don't Take Yourself So Seriously!

Someone once said that the most common disease in the world is "I" trouble. I saw an example of this one day after I had competed in a beauty pageant. I didn't win the pageant, but I did have a lot of fun. However, some of the other girls acted as if their lives were over because they didn't win! One of them had competed in this same pageant eight years in a row—always coming up just a little short. The morning after the pageant, she wore a T-shirt that pretty much summed up her attitude: "IT'S ALL ABOUT ME!"

It's easy to get bummed out when we live our lives that way! I once saw a poster that said: "Those who are wrapped up in themselves make a very small package." God wants to "unwrap us" from our self-centeredness so we can take an interest in the needs of others.

People with healthy self-esteem have learned not to take themselves too seriously. They aren't overly sensitive or thin-skinned when people joke about them or offer constructive criticism. They realize that they aren't the center of the universe.

A newly appointed Catholic bishop complained to Pope John XXIII that the burden of his new position prevented him from sleeping. "Oh," said John kindly, "the very same thing happened to me in the first few weeks after I became pope. But then one day my guardian angel appeared to me in a daydream and whispered, 'John, don't take yourself so seriously!' And ever since then I've been able to sleep."

When you quit taking yourself so seriously, you will be able to sleep better too. You'll live at peace with yourself, and most of the time with those around you. You can stop trying so hard to get positive feedback from others.

E'NEMY #3—

THE MANNEQUIN MISTAKE

And let us consider how we may spur one
another on toward love and good deeds.
—*Hebrews 10:24*

Once I took a modeling course. At the end of the course we were given a special assignment: to do "mannequin modeling" at our city's most high-class mall. Maybe you've never heard of mannequin modeling—I hadn't either. It means putting on whatever clothes are to be modeled and then standing *motionless* for hours so customers can stare at you.

When I first heard of the mannequin-modeling assignment, I thought it would be pretty cool. After all, not *everyone* gets to model at one of the city's fanciest department stores. And it would be nice to be seen in some of the sharpest outfits that money could buy.

However, after the first ten minutes, the thrill was gone. I found out how hard it is to stand absolutely still for a long time. And it was even *harder* for me because I tend to be highly social and a little hyperactive. Instead of just being a "pretty face" for the mall customers to look at, I wanted to talk to people. As I told my friends later, "Only a *dummy* would want to be a mannequin model!"

What's the Problem?

Ever since my experience as a mannequin model, I have wondered why it was such a downer. After all, I got to model the latest fashions in an upscale department store. I think it just made me realize how it would feel to be a person who doesn't know how to relate to people.

I once knew a girl named Cindy who was extremely pretty. Wherever she went, all eyes (especially the boys') turned her way. She could have been on the cover of any magazine. However, Cindy had little personality and virtually no ambition in life. Even though the boys were all attracted to her initially, when they got to know her, they found out that there wasn't much beneath her stunning outward beauty. She was like a book with a beautiful cover but very little content.

You might be the most beautiful person in the world, but you can't afford to be shallow! Take time to read a newspaper from time to time, not just the latest teen magazine. Read a book. Watch a news program occasionally. Find ways to expand your mind and not just beautify your body. Don't forget to develop your inner beauty.

Mannequins Get Depressed

Of course, there are many outwardly beautiful people who are inwardly beautiful as well. But what about mannequins (those who have outer beauty but no inner substance)? You might think that it can't be true, but many mannequins are depressed. Why? One of the reasons is that self-esteem is more closely linked to *what we accomplish in life* and *what we do to help other people* than it is to how we look.

One of the best ways to develop as a person of substance and avoid depression is to reach out to others who are in need. As we get our eyes off of ourselves, it's amazing how much better we feel! Corrie ten Boom, who survived a Nazi concentration camp during World War II, once said:

> Look around . . . and be distressed.
>
> Look within . . . and be depressed.
>
> But look at Jesus . . . and be at rest!

Author Neil Eskelin writes, "People with low self-esteem are almost always self-centered and preoccupied with their own thoughts and actions. Instead of asking, 'What can I do for you?' they ask, 'What do you think of *me*?' They constantly look outside themselves for a source of validation."

Dr. Karl Menninger, a famous psychiatrist, was asked after one of his lectures, "What would you advise a person to do if he felt a nervous breakdown coming on?" Most of the people expected him to reply, "Consult a psychiatrist." To their surprise, he had quite a different answer: "Lock up your house, go across the railway tracks, find someone in need, and do something to help that person."

My grandmother, Nan Buchan, was a good example of this principle. She went through some rough times in her life, but she had a strategy for the days when she was feeling the most discouraged. Instead of giving in to self-pity, she would find someone else who was even more discouraged than she was. Time and again, I was amazed by how well this strategy worked. As she got her eyes off of herself and found needy people to encourage, she went away uplifted and feeling much better about her own situation. She had discovered a great key to a healthy self-image.

My grandmother followed an important truth in the Bible: "Do nothing out of selfish ambition or vain conceit, but in humility consider others better than yourselves. Each of you should look not only to your own interests, but also to the interests of others" (Philippians 2:3–4). "And let us consider how we may spur one another on toward love and good deeds" (Hebrews 10:24). Instead of being content to be a good-looking mannequin, she chose to focus on helping others.

More Than a Pretty Face

When you go through hard times, you see that your life must consist of more than outward beauty or earthly possessions. Before Rebecca St. James became a popular Christian singer, her family went through a very difficult experience. They had just moved to America from Australia, and her dad lost his job. They were left without any money and weren't even sure what they were going to do for food. Their house had hardly any furniture, and they didn't own a car. But as they prayed, they saw God do many miracles. They learned to trust him, and he met their needs.

During this time, Rebecca learned one of the great lessons of life: the value of being a servant instead of expecting everyone to serve her. She and her family made money by doing such things as cleaning houses, babysitting, and raking leaves. Not very glamorous work for a future singing star! But it helped Rebecca make one of the greatest discoveries of her life. "Until we give ourselves away," she concluded, "we never truly discover who God wants us to be."

Someone once said, "When we forget ourselves, we usually do something everyone else remembers." That has surely been true for Rebecca St. James, and it can happen for us as well. However, it means we have to get out of the mannequin window and become involved in helping others. Albert Einstein, the famous scientist, once said, "Only a life lived for others is a life worthwhile."

Some of the greatest experiences in my life have come when I followed God's direction in giving my life away to others. Mission trips to Haiti and New Zealand, community service projects to help the poor, and outreaches to nursing homes and pregnancy distress centers have given me great joy in being a giver and not just a taker.

ENEMY #4—

FALSE EXPECTATION FRUSTRATION

It is better to take refuge in the LORD
than to trust in man.
—Psalm 118:8

My friend Amber was very popular in her new school. One of the hottest guys asked her out, and the popular girls invited her to their parties. I had never seen her so happy!

But suddenly all that changed. Her boyfriend found someone new. If that wasn't bad enough, he spread lies and turned even her best friends against her. Within days, she went from being one of the most popular girls in school to having virtually no friends at all. Amber was *very* upset.

What can we learn from Amber's sad experience? Have you ever had a time when people told you how wonderful you were one day and then drop you the next day like a hot potato? Do you know what it's like to have a soaring self-esteem when everybody likes you, but then feel lower than a worm when everyone turns on you?

Every kid has felt rejected at one time or another. Sometimes it's only our twisted thinking inspired by the image we see in the House of Mirrors. We overreact; we take things too personally. But what about situations when the rejection is real, like it was with Amber?

Basing our self-esteem on how popular we are with others is a dangerous thing to do. Why? Because, as we all know, popularity comes and goes. Even our best friends and closest relatives will let us down sometimes. If we tie our self-esteem to that, we'll be on one big roller coaster ride!

Getting Off the Roller Coaster

If you find that your life has all the wild ups and downs of a roller coaster, you may be looking too much to other people to nurture your self-esteem. As you've probably figured out on your own, that doesn't work too well—unless, of course, you like all those heart-stopping highs and stomach-turning lows. People mean well, but they usually end up disappointing us in some way or other.

So, if you shouldn't base your self-esteem on what other people think, what should you base it on? Your self-image should be grounded on a conviction in your heart, rather than the opinion of others. It should be something *internal* (in your heart), rather than something *external* (other people).

If your self-esteem bounces up and down faster than a ball of flubber, it's clear that you've attached it to changeable opinions and circumstances instead of anchoring it to unchanging truths about yourself. If you get depressed whenever your friends don't call you as often as you think they should, your self-esteem needs a firmer anchor.

Okay, I realize that nobody has a self-image that's up all the time. It's hard to keep from being affected by how others treat us. But please don't let that be the main source of your self-image, or you'll find yourself getting frustrated all the time.

Eggs in One Basket

When we lived in Florida, my sister Abby had a best friend named Maria. Maria lived next door, and she and Abby were always together. With Maria around, Abby didn't feel much of a need to build friendships with other girls. After all, she and Maria always had a blast together. Why would Abby need anyone else?

Then one day Maria decided she wanted to hang out with Allison, who lived down the street. Maria and Abby hadn't had a fight or anything, but Maria wanted to spend the day with someone else.

This was very hard for Abby. How could Maria do such a thing to her? Abby felt totally rejected and couldn't figure out what she had done wrong. Over-reacting, Abby said that Maria would probably never be her friend again.

Abby had "put all her eggs in one basket." Her self-esteem was much too wrapped up in her friendship with Maria. Feelings of rejection came not because Maria was actually mad at her, but simply because Abby had wrong expectations of their relationship.

What Do You Expect?

It's important to be honest about the expectations we have of others. Do you expect your friends to always meet your needs, boost your self-esteem, and be there when you have a problem? Sorry, but you're setting yourself up for disappointment.

I once had a friend named Sarah who was very possessive. If she called me and I wasn't there, she would ask, "Where's Molly?" and "Do you know when she's coming home?" By her tone of voice, it was clear that she was upset because I wasn't there to take her call. And although I enjoyed spending time with her, she sometimes got irritated when I wanted to spend time with other people as well.

Sarah had expectations that I simply couldn't meet. I wasn't about to sit all day by my phone waiting for her call. Nor was I willing to make her my only friend. If Sarah felt rejected by me at times, it was simply because her expectations were unreasonable.

I learned a lot from my relationship with Sarah. I saw that I, too, often have unreasonable expectations. Acting as if I were the center of the universe, I expected them to cater to my every need. When that didn't happen, I felt angry and depressed. My self-esteem sank, and I felt like they didn't love me or value me—even though that was the furthest thing from the truth. Author Ethel Barrett was right when she said, "We would worry less about what others think of us if we realized how seldom they do."

Sometimes our unrealistic expectations are targeted at our parents or family members. Treating them as if they are our genie or butler, we expect them to always be available to solve our problems or give us a ride, money, or emotional support. When they don't meet our demands, we pout and feel neglected.

It's time to give our parents a break. They don't have an easy job! We need to understand that it's unreasonable to expect our parents—or anyone—to be perfect. To do so is a sure way to get frustrated.

People will let us down at times. But we can always count on Jesus. The Bible says, "Whoever believes in him will not be disappointed" (Romans 10:11 NASB).

Enemy #5—

The People-Pleasing Pit

Am I now trying to win the approval of men,
or of God?
Or am I trying to please men?
If I were still trying to please men,
I would not be a servant of Christ.
—Galatians 1:10

I got into some major trouble one day when I was twelve years old and my parents left me with a babysitter. I actually took my dad's car and drove to pick up his boss's daughter. You can imagine how shocked I was when I got there and my dad's boss just happened to be standing outside in the driveway! Can you believe it? There I was, with my mouth wide open and totally embarrassed.

My dad's boss was not amused. Neither were my parents when they got home. I'll never forget what my dad said when he heard the news: "Molly, I'm very disappointed in you."

Whether we admit it or not, we all like to please other people. I felt bad that I let my parents down that day. I know I've disappointed them many times, but in my heart I want to please them. I want them to be proud of me.

Even though people-pleasing is one of the deadly enemies of healthy self-esteem, there are times when we need to listen to what other people say to us—like our parents, teachers, and pastors. Sometimes a desire to please people can help us do the right things in our lives.

But it's important to remember that we can't please everyone all the time. It just isn't possible to make everyone around us happy. We can't let other people's opinions define us or shape our self-image. Our goal in life should be to please God.

Peer Pressure

Nothing is more destructive than giving in to negative peer pressure. A lot of kids sell out to alcohol, drugs, cigarettes, and premarital sex, thinking that will make them popular with the "in" crowd. It might temporarily. But ultimately, giving in to peer pressure will actually *weaken* your self-esteem.

Have you learned this yet? Have you discovered that when you do things you shouldn't do, you never feel better about yourself, only worse? You can't improve your self-image by letting other people squeeze you into their molds.

By letting ourselves get talked into doing stuff we know is wrong, we're making ourselves slaves to other people and often to destructive habits as well. Slaves don't have much self-esteem! On the other hand, you will be amazed to find out how much your self-image will be strengthened when you stand up and do what you know is right. I changed when I finally decided to let God's image of me become my self-image.

It might be hard at first to change, especially if you've been going along with the crowd. But every time you stand up and do what's right, you'll feel stronger. It won't be as hard to say no the next time.

If you still find yourself losing the battle against peer pressure, that shows that your self-esteem is low. If you truly valued yourself, you wouldn't sell yourself so cheaply!

Instead of being so concerned about pleasing our friends, we need to grow in our desire to please God. The apostle Paul said, "So we make it our goal to please him . . ." (2 Corinthians 5:9). That's a good goal to have! Paul also kept this in mind when he was praying for his Christian friends: "And we pray this in order that you may live a life worthy of the Lord and may please him in every way: bearing fruit in every good work, growing in the knowledge of God . . ." (Colossians 1:10).

Someday we will all appear before the throne of God. On that day, it won't matter what our friends think about us. Only God's opinion will matter. Jesus warned the people of his day that they were on dangerous ground if they spent their time trying to get approval from people more than from God: "How can you believe if you accept praise from one another, yet make no effort to obtain the praise that comes from the only God?" (John 5:44).

Get Ready, Here It Comes

You don't need to be a brain surgeon to realize that temptations to compromise are sure to come your way from time to time. You need to get ready *ahead of time.* You can fight those feelings of wanting to give in and do something with your friends that you know you shouldn't. The following questions will help you form a battle plan.

?? **If someone offers you drugs, what will you say?**

?? **If a boy wants to kiss you and you don't want him to, do you know how to say no?**

?? **If you're at a slumber party, and someone sneaks in beer, how will you handle the situation?**

?? **If a friend encourages you to try a cigarette, what will you do?**

?? **If a friend wants you to shoplift, how can you have the courage to say no?**

?? **If someone wants to copy your homework, what will you say?**

Instead of waiting until something like this happens, decide now how you will react in those situations. What does this have to do with self-esteem? Everything! You will never have a healthy image of yourself if you go around with a guilty conscience all the time.

What to Do with Criticism

So how does a girl with healthy self-esteem handle criticism? There are two important ways:

1. *A girl with a healthy self-image won't believe every negative comment that comes her way. If*

someone calls her ugly, stupid, or a big fat failure, she doesn't automatically believe it! She knows that God doesn't see her that way. She knows that he loves her and wants her to know just how much.

2. *A girl with a healthy self-image will recognize that there's always room for growth, and she is eager for helpful advice from others.* Let's face it, we all have "blind spots"—areas of our lives that look fine to us but which need a little polishing. We all need real friends who can tell us the truth, even if we don't like hearing it. Instead of getting angry, we need to think about what they have to say. Painful? You bet! Helpful? Without a doubt!

Do you have a friend who loves you enough to be straight with you? I'm not talking about someone who likes to put you down, but someone who cares enough about you to tell you the truth about who you are. That's a real friend.

Flattery Isn't Your Friend!

Although our self-image can be harmed if we don't know what to do with the criticism that comes our way, flattery is just as destructive. Just as it's dangerous to believe every critical remark, it's also dangerous to believe all the *good* things people say about us. A person who wants something from us will often flatter us and tell us anything we want to hear. It may feel good at the time, but it can be a real trap.

Flattery can be especially dangerous when it comes from a boy. I bet you wouldn't mind hearing comments like, "You're the most beautiful girl in the world!" or "You have such an incredible personality!" or "I've never met a girl like you!" It's not likely you'll hear those remarks from a boy your own age, but you might from an older guy. Watch out!

Just as destructive criticism isn't based on the truth of who you are, flattery isn't based on the truth either. I've had friends who listened to older guys "sweet talk" them and soon they had "fallen in love." You're too young to fall in love! Start praying now for the guy God would like you to marry someday. In the meantime, it's more fun to just be friends.

Are You Vulnerable?

A girl with low self-esteem is much more vulnerable to criticism and flattery. Every little nasty remark can bring on tears, and the person who says something nice often becomes her best friend.

My dad once told me a story about something that took place when he was a teenager. His church youth group visited a nearby lake and a new girl named Connie came with them. Connie had been sick during most of her childhood and had spent a lot of time in doctors's offices and hospitals. She couldn't attend school and had no friends.

As the youth group was getting ready to return to the church, Connie tripped over a rock and fell. Tom, a long-haired ex-drug addict, happened to be standing close by at the time, so he reached out his hand to help Connie up. That wouldn't have been much of an event for most people, but Connie told Tom, "That was the nicest thing anyone has ever done for me!" Like Miss Piggy in the Muppet movies, she got stars in her eyes and immediately fell "in love" with Tom.

Why would someone respond like that to a simple act of kindness? Connie's self-esteem was so low that even the most basic kindness seemed romantic. Although Tom had done nothing more than what anyone nearby would have done, Connie's heart cried out, "He loves me!"

If you suffer from a poor self-image and are starved for love, be careful that you don't misunderstand the kind gestures of others. You could easily be selling yourself short.

God wants you to know that you're valuable and special because he created you. You don't need to fit in with the "in" crowd to be worth something. Just be you. It's the God thing to do!

Enemy #6—
Victim Valley

As they pass through the Valley of Baca [Weeping],
they make it a place of springs.
—Psalm 84:6

I met a girl named Jenny at a party one night. After introducing myself, I casually asked her how she was doing, but I wasn't ready for her answer.

Two and a half hours later, Jenny was just completing her whole life story. She probably would have kept going, but I told her it was getting close to my curfew and I had to leave.

Jenny had been sexually abused by a relative. Although the abuse happened years earlier, it was still fresh in her mind, and she wanted to make sure I knew all about it. Instead of telling me about the good things that had happened in her life since then, she focused on how she had been victimized. As a result, she had become a negative, bitter, and critical person—not much fun to be around.

As I left the party, I couldn't help thinking how odd it was for Jenny to tell me her whole life story when I merely asked her how she was doing. I was a total stranger to her, and she certainly had not made a very positive impression. What had happened to her was horrible, but by the end of the conversation I wanted to scream at the top of my lungs, "Get over it!" or "Quit feeling sorry for yourself!"

What's a Person to Do?

Maybe you think I'm being too hard on Jenny. After all, abuse is pretty awful. It can leave deep scars.

But let's look at the big picture: *Everyone* could claim to be a victim of *something*! Perhaps it isn't sexual abuse, but maybe we come from a broken home or have health problems. Or maybe the abuse we've suffered is verbal—our parents or siblings are constantly putting us down. In some cases, the abuse might have been neglect or abandonment.

Although it's likely that everyone has visited "Victim Valley" at one time or another, we need to be careful about not camping there for too long!

The trauma may have been very real and painful, but we can't allow ourselves to get "stuck" in the victim role. The Bible gives the fantastic promise that those who walk through the Valley of Weeping can turn it into a place of springs (Psalm 84:6).

Here are some keys I've discovered to escape from Victim Valley:

! *Forgive, forgive, forgive.* Even though it may actually feel good to hold grudges, they will eventually eat us up inside and make us bitter, self-centered sourpusses.

! *Focus on the future, not the past.* When we refuse to stop focusing on past traumas, we are like a person trying to drive a car while looking only in the rearview mirror. The House of Mirrors is full of rearview mirrors!

! *Quit using victimhood as a way to get attention.* As I saw while talking to Jenny, some people feel that the only way they can get people's attention is to tell a "Woe is me" story. We need to see that people can love us for who we are, apart from any need for sympathy.

! *Stop throwing pity parties.* When we constantly throw pity parties, we will soon discover that we are the only guest! We will find ourselves increasingly alone and isolated. No one wants to be around someone who's always whining and complaining.

! *Watch what you say.* Even if we struggle with feelings of being a victim, we need to be careful about sharing our negative perspective with everyone we meet (as Jenny did with me). People often gain their view of us from what we say about ourselves! If we're always putting ourselves down and saying things like, "I'm really ugly," "Nobody likes me," or "I'm such an idiot," we shouldn't be surprised when other people start saying those things about us too.

! *Cultivate an attitude of gratitude.* Regardless of what we've been through, we should learn to have a thankful heart. We all know someone who has endured a terrible situation but continues to be cheerful and uplifting. We don't have to be grouches just because we've gone through some tough times.

! *Reach out to others.* No matter what you've been through, someone somewhere has gone through worse. As we reach out to others in need, we find our own self-esteem rising. There's no surer way to escape from Victim Valley.

! *Get help.* By saying that we can "get over it" and get on with our lives, I'm not suggesting that we merely bury our problems and ignore them. Sometimes we've suffered traumas so great that we need to find a skilled counselor who can help us in the recovery process. But be careful. It's important to find someone who can point you toward the future without dwelling forever on the past.

Tear Up Your Fake ID Card!

Perhaps you've heard of underage kids who have gotten a fake ID card in order to get into bars or purchase alcohol. The fact of the matter is, most of us have a "fake ID" in one way or another. Instead of carrying around our true identity, we put forward a false impression of who we are.

This is particularly true of those who have become stuck in Victim Valley. The "ID card" Jenny handed me said "VICTIM" in big, dark letters. She was a physically attractive, intelligent, and healthy person. And yet she allowed all her good qualities to be buried under her sense of victimhood.

You don't need to accept the false IDs that people try to pin on you. If they hand you a "VICTIM" ID card—tear it up. If they hand you a "LOSER" ID card—tear it up. If they hand you an ID card that says "UNPOPULAR"—tear it up. If they try to label you with an "UGLY" ID card—tear it up. If the card they hand you says "BAD GIRL"—you know what to do! Tear it up!

There are lots of false ID cards in the House of Mirrors. But they aren't the real you! Tear them up today, and your self-esteem will soar to new heights. You are God's creation, and he doesn't make any junk! (See Ephesians 2:10; Psalm 139:13–14.)

ENEMY #7—
FAILURE FIXATION

All have sinned and fall short of the glory of God.
—Romans 3:23

When Jessica Simpson was twelve years old, she auditioned for the Mickey Mouse Club television program. After her talents took her all the way to the finals, Jessica freaked out during her last audition. "I froze," she laughs, "but the experience made me even stronger and more convinced that I was on the right path."

Britney Spears, Christina Aguilera, and Justin Timberlake each got a role in the Mickey Mouse Club that year, but not Jessica Simpson. She felt like a failure. She had blown her big opportunity.

The following year while attending church camp, Jessica sang an a cappella version of "Amazing Grace" for one of the camp's guest speakers who was in the process of launching a gospel music label. Jessica signed to the label and worked on an album for three years, but the small recording company folded before her CD was ever released. Again, it looked like Jessica had worked on her music in vain.

However, the setback didn't stop Jessica one bit. Using the songs she had worked on for her CD, she did concerts at Christian youth conferences and in churches. Before long, Jessica's reputation as a talented singer filtered out of the religious world and into the pop music realm. She was signed to a big contract with Capitol Records.

Jessica Simpson had many opportunities to get discouraged and give up, but she continued to persevere until she fulfilled her dream. When she saw Britney Spears, Christina Aguilera, Justin Timberlake, and others find fame and fortune, she could have gotten a bad attitude or gotten down on herself. But Jessica Simpson didn't focus on failure.

Does that mean that Jessica's days of failure and disappointment are behind her forever? No. No one succeeds in *everything* they try.

In 2000, Jessica faced a huge letdown when she was up for the Best New Artist Award at the American Music Awards. She had to fight back tears when the group Three Doors Down was announced as the winner. "I wanted it so bad I could taste it," Jessica admitted. "When I didn't win, I just sat in my chair and thought, *Jessica, you are such a failure!*"

Failing Doesn't Make You a Failure

As a result of her disappointments, Jessica Simpson learned one of the secrets to a healthy self-image: *Even though we all fail at times, that doesn't make us a failure.* The key is refusing to give up.

Jessica Simpson isn't the only person who failed many times before success came. Here are a few examples you might not know about:

! Basketball star Michael Jordan was cut from his high school basketball team at Laney High School in Wilmington, North Carolina.

! Right before her breakthrough CD was released, country singer Jo Dee Messina was on the verge of bankruptcy.

! Just five years before becoming the Super Bowl MVP, quarterback Kurt Warner's football career seemed washed up, and he took a job bagging groceries at a local store.

! **Thomas Edison tried more than a thousand unsuccessful experiments before inventing a workable electric light bulb.**

The common ingredient in each of these stories is that the person refused to give up, even after experiencing failure. While many might have been totally bummed and depressed, these people didn't allow their temporary failures to destroy their dreams or their self-esteem.

There has never been a book that explains failure as well as the Bible. Many of its greatest heroes experienced failure and disappointment, yet God helped them get on their feet again. We are promised that those who are in Christ become new creations (2 Corinthians 5:17). Our old life—failures and all—passes away, and we are given a whole new beginning. Pretty amazing deal, huh?

From Setbacks to a Cosmetics Empire

Maybe you've never heard of the late Mary Kay Ash, but you've probably heard of Mary Kay Cosmetics. Maybe you've seen one of the pink Cadillacs the organization gives to their top salespersons.

One day Mary Kay told her attorney of her dream to start a cosmetics business that would give every woman who worked in it unlimited opportunities for advancement. He thought she was crazy. "Mary Kay," he said, "if you are going to throw away your life savings, why don't you just go directly to the trash can? It will be much easier than what you are proposing." Her accountant didn't offer her any hope either.

Nevertheless, Mary Kay moved ahead toward her dream. She sank her entire life savings—$5,000—into her new business. She put her husband in charge of the administrative side of things while she worked hard to prepare the products and training materials. They were making wonderful progress until tragedy struck just a month before they were planning to open for business. Mary Kay's husband died of a heart attack right at their kitchen table.

Most people would have accepted defeat after a blow like that. But not Mary Kay. By the year 2000, the cosmetics business, which started in 1963, had global wholesale sales of $1.2 billion and empowered 750,000 salespeople in 37 countries worldwide. It's a good thing Mary Kay didn't give up!

What to Do When You Mess Up

Some of the setbacks we face in life are not just "unfortunate situations," but rather the result of our own poor choices. Our *reaction* to our mistakes will often determine whether we become focused on our failure or use it to learn something that will help us succeed later.

Here are four keys that will help you avoid getting stuck in a never-ending cycle of failure:

✔ *Forgive yourself.* If you're still punishing yourself for some past failure, stop it! No good can come of beating yourself up over something that happened in the past. God has promised to forgive you if you ask him to, so there's no reason not to forgive yourself.

✔ *Focus on your achievements, not on your shortcomings.* We all have plenty of shortcomings. But you will never overcome yours by dwelling on them. Instead, focus on your successes, your dreams, and the good qualities in your life. This is one of the most important lessons for cultivating a healthy self-image.

✔ *Remember that failure isn't final—tomorrow is a brand-new day.* If you've been locked in the grip of failure and frustration, determine that when you wake up tomorrow morning, you will start with a clean slate. Instead of carrying your past failures around with you, decide now to give yourself a fresh start. As the saying goes, "Today is the first day of the rest of your life!"

- ✔ **_Learn from your mistakes._** When we refuse to learn our lessons from our failures, our mistakes are turned into _habits_. Someone once said, "Our mistakes start as small as cobwebs, but if we continue in them, they become like cables." One of the best ways to learn from your mistakes is to ask for help from faithful friends who love you enough to tell you the truth.

- ✔ **_Be willing to take risks again._** When I was only ten, I was scheduled to sing a solo at both of the Sunday morning services at our church. At the early service, I was _terrible_, getting so nervous that I completely sang the wrong melody! After that humiliating experience, I never wanted to sing in public again—but the second service was coming. Despite my fears, I gave it a try, and this time it went fantastic. My success only came when I was willing to risk failing again.

Your Time to Bat Is Coming!

The story has been told of a man in Los Angeles who was walking past a vacant lot where some seven- and eight-year-old boys were playing baseball. He asked one of the boys, "What's the score?"

"We're behind eighteen to nothing," the boy answered cheerfully.

"Well," said the man, "you certainly don't look discouraged."

"Discouraged?" replied the boy. "Why would we be discouraged? We haven't even come to bat yet!"

Think about it. Regardless of what happened in the past, today is a new ball game. You are coming to bat. This is your time to win!

ENEMY #8—

TOXIC RELATIONSHIP RUTS

*Do not be misled: "Bad company
corrupts good character."*
—*1 Corinthians 15:33*

In the third grade Emily was one of my best
friends, but only for a while. She was really
popular and the kind of person who made you
feel good about yourself when she was your friend.
But I discovered that there was another side of
Emily: You never knew whether she would be your
best friend or your worst enemy.

On days when Emily was my best friend, it was
flattering that she would shut out everyone else and
focus her full attention on me. But I never knew
when she would change her mind on the spur of
the moment and find a *new* best friend. Then she
would shut *me* out. With Emily you never knew

whether you were in or out. I didn't understand it at the time, but she was a "toxic" person.

I've seen many other toxic relationships over the years. My friend Annie dated a strange guy named Curtis. When she finally broke up with him, he sent a virus to her computer that completely erased all the information on her hard drive! His self-esteem must not have been able to handle the crushing blow of being dumped by the girl of his dreams. His reaction showed that the relationship wasn't based on true love and respect. It had been toxic all along.

My friend Katie dated a messed-up guy named Pete. When she tried to end the relationship, he stormed away and said he was going to kill himself! Katie and her mom were up until 3:00 in the morning trying to talk him out of ending his life. It turned out to be a toxic relationship.

Who Do You Hang Out With?

Hanging out with toxic people is bad for your self-esteem! A person with healthy self-esteem will tend to form healthy relationships. A person with a poor self-image will be more vulnerable to toxic relationships.

If you feel like a "loser," you will be more likely to hang out with other losers. If you feel like a champion, you will generally spend most of your time with other champions. How you select your friends says a lot about your self-esteem.

The Bible gives us lots of advice about how to choose our friends. The apostle Paul told the Corinthians, "Do not be misled: 'Bad company corrupts good character'" (1 Corinthians 15:33). He also wrote about the dangers of becoming deeply entangled in relationships with people who are not following Christ (2 Corinthians 6:14).

However, some of our toxic relationships may be ones that we have little control over. Perhaps you have a toxic relative or a teacher at school. You didn't choose to be involved with these people, but you have to learn to deal with them anyway.

One of my sixth-grade teachers, Mr. Davies, never liked me much. At the end of the school year, he gave out various awards to his students. The award he gave me was the "Daisy Duke" award, which was meant to imply that I am physically attractive, but stupid. Although this was meant to be funny, it really hurt my feelings. Mr. Davies was a toxic person, and all I could do was shake off his comments and make the best of the situation.

Some people seem to become addicted to toxic relationships. My friend Kaitlin's mom refuses to get away from her boyfriend, even though he beats her, takes all her money, and often gets busted by the police for selling cocaine and other drugs. Kaitlin's mom sometimes has separated from this jerk for a week or two, but she always goes back to him. Although he has become dangerous to both her and Kaitlin, she seems unable to break free from him.

Warning Signs

It's easy to say that we should do what we can to stay away from toxic people, but often we simply don't recognize the symptoms until we have already been hurt. If the unhealthy relationship has existed a long time, it will probably be even harder to recognize and harder to escape. As time goes on, the relationship becomes a rut.

Here are some common warning signs of the types of people who will cause us problems:

!# *People who are continually negative and critical about life. Do your best to spend time with people who are optimistic, positive, and uplifting (see Philippians 4:8).*

!# *People who enjoy gossiping about others.* Believe me, I've done my share of gossiping. But I've found that when I talk about people behind their backs, soon people will be talking about me behind my back. Often the very people I have gossiped to will end up gossiping about me. I've learned that sooner or later, I always reap what I sow (see Galatians 6:7).

!# *People who are two-faced and don't tell the truth.* If someone lies to you once, how do you know they won't lie to you a second or a third time? If you hear one of your friends lie to someone else, you should really wonder if next time he or she will lie to you.

!# *People who can't control their anger.* Everyone gets angry at one time or another, but it's not healthy to be around someone who frequently loses his or her temper. This kind of toxic relationship often ends in physical violence. Don't take the chance!

!# *People who try to draw us into harmful activities.* Let's be honest: Kids who try to get us to smoke, take drugs, shoplift, use profanity, or engage in pre-marital sex are not true friends. True friends are those who bring out the *best* in us, not those who cause us to lower ourselves to their standards.

!# *People who are possessive of our time and attention.* I once was in a youth group where there were three or four girls who were really close friends. But when I became best friends with one of the girls, Carrie, she drew me away from the others. She wanted all my time and attention, and pretty soon I'd lost my other friends. In our search for deep relationships, we need to be careful that we don't end up in a toxic friendship like this one. A healthy friendship is not an exclusive one—it sets us free to develop other close relationships.

!# *People who try to pull you down when you try to achieve something.* **When a bunch of crabs are put into a bucket, none of them can climb out. When one tries to climb out, the others all pull it back into the bucket. Don't limit yourself by what other people think about you or even what you yourself think you can accomplish. God has much more for you!**

How to Escape the Toxic Trap

What can you do if you find yourself in one or more relationships like the ones we've talked about here? Some toxic relationships are worse than others. Some are so dangerous that you need to cut off the relationship immediately. This takes courage, but you will feel a lot better about yourself once you have cut off relationships that are clearly having a negative effect on you.

In other cases, the relationship should be minimized but not cut off entirely. Your main strategy in such situations is to work on new, healthy relationships that will grow deeper and deeper as the toxic relationships become less important in your life.

A healthy self-image needs healthy soil to grow in. Even if you do everything else that I suggest in this book, your self-esteem will still suffer if you allow toxic relationships to dominate your life. Down in your heart you know that some kids bring out the best in you, while others bring out the worst. You like the person you become when you're around certain people, while others always leave you with lower self-esteem.

The choice is yours. Don't let your life become a toxic waste dump.

ENEMY #9—

PERFECTIONIST PARALYSIS

Not that I have already obtained all this,
or have already been made perfect,
but I press on to take hold of that for
which Christ Jesus took hold of me.
—Philippians 3:12

My friend Melissa grew up as an only child in a strict family. Her parents expected her to pretty much be perfect—straight A's in school, angelic behavior, a bedroom that was always clean, and outstanding performance in her music lessons and on her sports teams.

When Melissa was little, she tried to live up to these expectations. Yet as hard as she tried, it seemed that she was always falling short. Sometimes she got B's in school. Occasionally she got into mischief with the neighbor kids. Every once in a while, she forgot to make her bed. And sometimes she was not the best student in her music class or the best athlete on her sports teams.

When these "failures" occurred, Melissa's parents tried prodding her to do better. When that didn't work, they tried yelling at her and taking away privileges. But Melissa was doing the best she could.

Then something happened inside Melissa's head. She decided that if she couldn't be perfect and live up to her parent's standards, she might as well give up and quit trying. To her parent's shock, her grades fell to C's and some were worse. She announced that she wasn't going to take music lessons anymore or play sports.

Melissa's parents tried to get her to join the debate team or try out for the lead role in school musicals. What they didn't understand was that Melissa had made a decision in her heart: *If I can't be perfect at something, I won't try it at all.* The result, as we might expect, was that Melissa hardly ever tried anything new. It was too risky. She might not be perfect, and she had been taught that anything short of perfection was failure.

Melissa had fallen into the trap called "Perfectionist Paralysis." If she couldn't do something perfectly, she refused to do it at all. If she wasn't sure she could perform better than everyone else, she would just stay on the sidelines and watch. She wouldn't try anything that might lead to imperfection or failure. Her self-image was shaped by a faulty belief system: *If I can't be perfect, I have no value at all.*

Living in a Straightjacket

I once had a friend named Megan whose parents were rich. Their house was a mansion, and they were strict about taking care of it. To keep dirt from being brought into the house, Megan and her friends had to take off their shoes in the garage. Megan was never allowed to get a drink or eat snacks between meals because that could cause crumbs or dirty dishes.

One room in the house was kept so spotless that it was totally off limits to Megan. I was amazed to learn that she and her friends weren't even allowed to sit on her bed because that would rumple the covers! Once when I visited Megan, her mother vacuumed the carpet behind me because I had made foot imprints by walking on the perfectly swept carpet.

The result of all this was that Megan became a prisoner in her own house. Not only was it hard to bring her friends to visit, but Megan constantly walked on eggshells. She was afraid to relax in her own house. The strict rules had put her in a straightjacket.

Probably without meaning to, Megan's parents had given her the message that the house was more important than her and her friends. How would this make you feel? It hurt Megan's self-esteem, because she felt that her parents valued their house and other possessions far more than they valued her.

Most of us originally get our self-image from how we are treated by our parents. Usually this is positive. However, as we saw in the cases of Melissa and Megan, sometimes parents try to make their kids live up to a standard of perfection that only brings frustration and resentment. This is another House of Mirrors that distorts our self-image. If you find yourself in a situation like this, you may have to find out who you are and receive encouragement for your self-esteem from other sources.

Steps to Freedom

What can a person do to be released from the paralysis of perfectionism? Here are helpful steps:

✓ *Realize that no one is perfect.* We might as well get it straight right now, perfection is not an attainable goal. If we measure ourselves against a standard of perfection, we will only become depressed and hopeless. As the Bible reminds us, "All have sinned and fall short of the glory of God" (Romans 3:23). Author and speaker Barbara Johnson says it this way: "Christians sometimes have more trouble handling trouble than the world does, because we think we should be perfect. Not so. We are just forgiven."

✓ *Pursue excellence, not perfection.* The pursuit of excellence is a wonderful thing—but not the pursuit of perfection. The goal should not be perfection, but simply to be the best you can be. Even the apostle Paul, one of the greatest Christians who has ever lived, knew that he was certainly not perfect: "Not that I have already obtained all this, or have already been made perfect, but I press on to take hold of that for which Christ Jesus took hold of me" (Philippians 3:12).

✓ *Have friends you can be totally honest with.* We've probably all been stabbed in the back by a "friend" who couldn't keep a secret. But we need true friends with whom we can really share our hearts—warts and all.

Singer and author Sheila Walsh learned this the hard way: "I used to be far more concerned with being 'inspirational' than with being real. But I now sense that people in pain need to know that they are not alone in their struggles. I am not advocating a coast-to-coast spiritual pity party—far from it. Rather, I suggest that as we receive the help and comfort of Christ, we in turn take a risk and extend that same hope and comfort to others. This is not a time to hide behind walls and put on a brave face; this is a time to stand in the light with our wounds and our flaws."

✔ *Focus on the areas you really can change.* We would save ourselves a lot of trouble if we could stop worrying about things that are impossible to change. Reinhold Niebuhr shares this principle in his famous "Serenity Prayer": *God grant me the Serenity to accept the things I cannot change, the Courage to change the things I can, and the Wisdom to know the difference.*

Have you come to know the difference between the things you can change about your life and the things you can't? Low self-esteem often comes from not accepting the things we can't change and not devoting ourselves to changing the things that can truly be improved.

Find Your Unique Niche!

When I was only three years old, my mom enrolled me in a Suzuki piano course. I have a pretty musical family, and I guess giving me piano lessons seemed like the logical thing to do. Starting with "Twinkle, Twinkle" and other exciting songs, I ended up taking the piano lessons for more than four years.

So how did I do? Not very well. To this day, I *hate* the piano! My sister Abby, on the other hand, loves musical instruments like a fish loves water. Go figure.

Even though I never made it as a pianist, I found that I had other talents. I loved my dance lessons and became a good volleyball player. But, as my parents will tell you, my greatest skill of all is talking on the phone!

There is a lesson here: We each need to find our own special, God-given gifts and abilities. Some things we will naturally be good at, while other things will be more of a struggle for us. Our self-esteem will become stronger when we focus on the areas where we are uniquely gifted. We still won't be perfect, but that's okay—no one else is either.

Enemy #10—

The Comfort-Zone Coffin

Have I not commanded you?
Be strong and courageous.
Do not be terrified; do not be discouraged,
for the LORD your God will be with you wherever you go.
—Joshua 1:9

I had a horrible time when I started at a new middle school one year. Some of the popular girls felt threatened that their boyfriends were interested in me, and a major battle broke out. They spread all kinds of rumors about me, and it didn't take long before I lost all my friends. After being there only half a year, things were so bad that my parents took me out of school and home schooled me for a while.

Being away from that middle school was a relief, and we decided that Metrolina Christian Academy would be a better place for me during the coming school year. There was only one problem: My experience at my old school was so terrible that I was afraid it would all happen again at Metrolina.

I didn't know what to do. Should I just keep home schooling, so I wouldn't have to face the stress of peer pressure and popularity games? Should I attend the new school but stay to myself and try not to get close to anyone? Should I try to give my personality a major makeover, hoping that I wouldn't be rejected next time?

I can tell you from my own experience that when your self-esteem has been damaged, it may take some time to restore it. It will also take courage. You may feel like backing away from people and curling up in a ball on your bed. You will have to be willing to take a chance again, to reach out in the very areas in which you feel the most insecure.

It's normal to feel fearful at times, but there is a solution—knowing that God is with you. Look at this great promise he gives us, "So do not fear, for I am with you; do not be dismayed, for I am your God. I will strengthen you and help you; I will uphold you with my righteous right hand" (Isaiah 41:10). You might have to face some difficult situations, but God wants to hold your hand and walk with you through it all.

A Frightening Journey

One day the Lord told Abraham (then known as Abram) to leave his relatives, friends, and home country and "go to the land I will show you" (Genesis 12:1). Wow! Now that's leaving your comfort zone! It's bad enough if we have to move and we know where we're headed, but Abraham "obeyed and went, even though he did not know where he was going" (Hebrews 11:8).

God seems to like to shake up our security from time to time so that we will learn to place our security in him. After spending my first nine years in Ohio, I have moved twice, first to Florida and then to North Carolina. Each time meant leaving my friends, school, church, and activities behind. But I like the conclusion that Moses made in Psalm 90:1: "Lord, you have been our dwelling place throughout all generations." Wherever our journey takes us, the Lord himself is our true dwelling place—our true security. He has promised to be with us.

The Christian life can sometimes seem like a terrifying journey. The Bible calls it a pilgrimage: "Blessed are those whose strength is in you, who have set their hearts on pilgrimage" (Psalm 84:5). Yet, as scary as the journey may be, it is much better than the boring life of staying in our comfort zone. Rebecca St. James says, "It is only when we get out of our comfort zones and begin to live by faith, that we truly see God at work in and through our lives."

No Fear!

A popular fashion for T-shirts and other teen clothing in recent years has been the "No Fear" logo. Why did that touch such a nerve? Because fear is perhaps the number one enemy of a positive self-image. The Bible says, "Fear of man will prove to be a snare, but whoever trusts in the LORD is kept safe" (Proverbs 29:25).

Look how fear plays a role in nearly every one of the other enemies we have discussed. **Don't be afraid . . .**

☺ *To be yourself.* Instead of giving in to the Copycat Caper, you need to have the courage to be yourself. That means finding your own unique personality, talents, and lifestyle.

☺ *To reach out to others.* Rather than being content to be a wallflower or mannequin, find a way to reach out to help other people. If you've been rejected in the past, it may take some guts to reach out again.

But your self-esteem will grow only as you get your eyes off yourself and onto the needs of others. The Bible says, "There is no fear in love. But perfect love drives out fear" (1 John 4:18).

☺ *To make mistakes along the way.* Remember: No one is perfect! The biggest mistake you can make is to be paralyzed by the *fear* of making mistakes. Dare to take a chance. In her book *Boomerang Joy*, Barbara Johnson writes, "Don't be afraid of mistakes or defeats; they are building blocks for all your successes."

☺ *To be rejected at times.* I wish I could tell you that if you follow my advice in this book, you will never be rejected again. But that would obviously be a lie. Rejection will come at times, but don't allow it to make you a defensive and withdrawn person.

☺ *To let go of toxic relationships.* It can be scary to close the door on a toxic relationship. You might wonder, *Will the person get mad at me? Will he or she try to retaliate and do something to harm me or damage my reputation? Will I be able to find someone else to fill the hole left when the toxic person leaves?* Despite all the questions and fears that arise, you must have the courage to rid your life of relationships that poison your self-esteem.

☺ *To make changes that will give your life a whole new beginning! Sometimes we don't like our lives as they are, but are afraid of making any changes that would take us into new and unfamiliar territory. If you want to grow up, you must be willing to let go of your old ways and adopt some new ways.*

Can a Life Really Change?

Many kids feel hopeless and think their lives can never change. They feel they're doomed to be rejected and unpopular. They don't like their toxic relationships but don't know how to get rid of them. Maybe they've tried to make changes in the past, only to fall back into their old ways.

Believe me, there really is hope. I've had my struggles, but God has changed my life. He can change yours too!

On Purpose—
Finding Your Glass Slipper

We have different gifts,
according to the grace given us.
—Romans 12:6

You know the story. After a night of romantic dancing with the handsome prince, Cinderella suddenly realizes it's nearly midnight. Knowing that her carriage will soon turn back into a pumpkin, she quickly leaves the ball, only to leave one of her glass slippers on the palace steps. Fortunately, the prince is determined to find the girl of his dreams, the one who fits the glass slipper. He searches throughout his kingdom until finally he finds her—lovely Cinderella.

This is more than a fairy tale. We each have a "glass slipper," a God-designed place in this world that only we can fill. Perhaps you have already seen parts of this in your life. You might not have been dancing with a handsome prince, but you some-how experienced a taste of your destiny. You knew this was more than copying someone else's dream, for you had touched on something that was made especially for you.

An important key to healthy self-esteem is find-ing your special role in life. Instead of trying to fit into someone else's glass slipper, a wonderful peace comes when you find and wear your own. This is not usually something that happens quickly or easily, but is something that develops over time.

Entire books could be written on the subject of finding your gifts and purpose in life. Let me just give you a few important questions to ask yourself as you get started on your journey:

?? *Are you more comfortable with people or with tasks? This is not necessarily an either/or issue, but each of us will have a tendency to go in one direction or the other. Some people find great enjoyment interacting with other people, but some would rather read a book or work by themselves on a creative project of some kind.*

As you think about the kinds of things you want to do in life, this is a very important question to ask yourself. If you are a "people person" who gets stuck in a task-oriented job, you will struggle. You will be wearing someone else's glass slipper, and it will give you blisters.

?? *Are you more comfortable being a leader, a manager, or a servant?* Before looking at these three functions, let me emphasize that *each* one of them is very important. Don't judge your importance by the role you identify with. And realize that your role may change as you grow older.

In general, leaders are those who have special ideas for the direction that needs to be taken, and a special ability to motivate others to follow. Managers are not as good at deciding the overall direction, but have more ability to put the ideas into action. Servants are not as comfortable making decisions about which way to go, but mostly want to work in a support role for the leaders and managers.

?? *What is the special area where you can make a positive impact?* Some kids are naturally artistic and creative. They are most likely to make their mark in an area like music, writing, inventing, or art. Others are naturally talented in sports. There are also some people who love learning for learning's sake. They are often the most successful in jobs that require a strong love for science or math. Your past successes will show you the areas you should focus on in the future.

Who are your heroes? Often we can learn a lot about ourselves by looking at our heroes. Those we admire the most may provide a clue to the things we want to do in life. For example, if your doctor is one of the "coolest" people you know, perhaps you would enjoy helping the sick and needy. If you have been greatly helped by one of your teachers at school, you may find yourself considering a career in teaching. If the pastor of your church is one of your heroes, maybe you would enjoy a position in ministry.

What do your closest friends and relatives tell you about your special talents? If people are always telling you, "You really should think about a career in music" or "You sure would make a great lawyer," take note. They might be right! On the other hand, don't be surprised if some of those around you try to discourage you from the very dream God has placed in your heart. Most successful people have to overcome lots of critics along the way.

What do you find particular joy in doing? Sometimes we make things much too hard when considering what we want to do in life. Often the answer can be found in simply figuring out what we really like to do. If you can do something that gives you

great fulfillment, and find a way to get paid for it, you are on your way to a wonderful life. You have discovered your glass slipper.

Trial and Error

I wish I could honestly tell you that after you answer these questions a light bulb will suddenly turn on in your head and you will instantly shout out, "That's it! I see my glass slipper!" That might happen for some of you, but usually the process isn't quite that easy. Instead of giving you foolproof direction for your future, these questions will mainly help you narrow down your options.

Perhaps you have an interest in some things you don't yet know much about. Although it might not sound very exciting, one of the best ways to find your glass slipper is by trial and error. That means you'd better get off the couch, turn off the TV for a while, and try different kinds of skills until you find the one that best suits you.

Trial and error often means falling on your face a few times, but that's part of the process. You may not have heard of Catherine Hicks, but she plays the mom on the TV show *Seventh Heaven*. Her dream as a teen was to be a college cheerleader at Notre Dame. When she didn't make the cheerleading squad, she was crushed. But when she looked out the window of her college dorm, she happened to see the drama building and decided to try out for a play. She got the part, and she is now a successful actress—all because she never made the cheerleading squad.

You can't afford to stay in your comfort zone if you really want to find your glass slipper. It often takes moving out into unfamiliar territory.

Find Out More

You also may need to do some research. The Internet is full of information on all sorts of careers, and there are also some great books in the library. Your guidance counselor at school may offer some personality and skills tests that can point you toward your true interests.

Some of the best research is simply asking questions of those who are already working in the type of career you're considering. If you're interested in working with the FBI, it would be a good idea to talk to someone who works there. If you think it would be fun to be a veterinarian, find one who will answer the questions you have.

Okay, you may be saying, "I'm just a kid! Why should I think about what I'll be doing later in life?" Well, I agree that you surely don't want to spend *all* your time figuring out your future career. But you might find it more enjoyable to work on this than you think. You are never too young to get started!

Learn by Serving

One of the best ways to find our special role in life is by serving others. The more we do this, the more we'll discover the things we're really good at. The Bible encourages us to find our special gifts by serving others with God's love: "Each one should use whatever gift he has received to serve others, faithfully administering God's grace in its various forms" (1 Peter 4:10).

That might surprise you. Maybe you thought you could find your special place in this world by focusing more on yourself. But it doesn't work that way. We learn more about ourselves as we take our eyes off of ourselves and find ways that we can be a help to those around us. As we do that, our special gifts will soon be clear.

You'll Know It When You See It

Cinderella could have stayed home the night of the ball. She could have complained that she had nothing to wear and felt hopeless about all the obstacles put in her way by her wicked stepmother and stepsisters. Yet Cinderella didn't give up. She heard destiny calling and wasn't willing to take no for an answer. She used every stumbling block as a steppingstone to reach her goal.

You might not yet know what you should do with your life. It might be hard to picture right now. But God wants to help you. He has a great plan for your life. As you learn to pray and keep your eyes open to his leading, you will recognize your glass slipper when you see it.

Don't be afraid to dance with your destiny. God has created a glass slipper just for you!

ACTIVATION—
NOW GO AHEAD AND SHINE!

*In the same way, let your light shine before men,
that they may see your good deeds
and praise your Father in heaven.*
—Matthew 5:16

Most people are surprised when I tell them that those who are wrapped up in themselves will not have a healthy self-image. The more self-centered we are, the more fault we will find with ourselves, and the more obnoxious we will be to others.

I heard a clever statement about this recently: "Most people live their lives like a fast-food restaurant: self-service only." The goal of positive self-esteem is not to be wrapped up in ourselves, but to be healthy, happy people who can reach out to others.

The Bible tells us that we should shine brightly, bringing light to a dark world: "Do everything without complaining or arguing, so that you may become blameless and pure, children of God without fault in a crooked and depraved generation, in which you shine like stars in the universe as you hold out the word of life" (Philippians 2:14–16). You can't be much of a beacon of light to others unless you have allowed God to fill you with his love.

Contrary to what you might have expected, if we have a good self-image, we will not be stuck-up or cocky. Nor will we put others down in order to lift ourselves up. We'll look for opportunities to serve and encourage those around us.

When we have a positive self-image and set out to make the world a better place for others, something amazing happens: Our self-esteem grows even more. So don't stop with just thinking better about yourself—find others to lift up too. Shine the light of God's love far and wide, and you'll never again lack healthy self-esteem. You can throw away your faulty mirrors, because you will have discovered who you really are.

Young Woman of Faith

Girlz Want to Know

Answers to Real-Life Questions

Susie Shellenberger

"If you enjoyed reading Take It from Me, then you'll love Girlz Want to Know!"

Zonderkidz

Section One

Questions About Family

Q. My dad was recently diagnosed with cancer. Sometimes he's in a lot of pain. He works a lot, and when he is home, it seems as if he and my mom are always going on walks together. I need him, too!

A. I'm so sorry your dad is fighting the tough battle of cancer. He's probably frightened and wondering how much time he has left. That must be scary for you as well.

If his days are numbered, he may be spending more time with your mom to ensure that everything's taken care of. For example, they may be talking about insurance, savings, the money for your future college years, etc. He probably wants to make sure your family will be well provided for after he's gone. And they may feel it's inappropriate, or too disturbing, to include you and your brothers or sisters in these conversations.

And though it seems he's spending extra time with your mom, he may not even realize that the two of you haven't had much time together recently. Why not bake his favorite dessert? Or rent one of his all-time fave videos, make some popcorn, and curl up on the couch with him.

Ask if the two of you can have a dad-daughter date, and tell him how much you love him. Meanwhile, since you know he's in physical pain, pray for him and be patient with him.

Q. Every person in my family is or was addicted to something. Can that be passed down in the genes?

A. Yes and no. Let's take it slow and simple, okay? There *is* such a thing as having a predisposition to addiction. That means you may have tendencies toward addiction. But if you know that, you can certainly learn to make wise choices to stay away from addictive things.

We all have free choice. Your family may be predisposed toward addictive behavior, but that doesn't mean there's no hope. You don't *have* to become addicted.

God doesn't want anyone to be addicted to anything. Have you asked him for help? Why don't we pray about it right now, okay?

Dear Jesus:

It makes me sad that everyone in my family is, or has been, addicted to something. I don't want to become an addict. Will you take control of my life? I want to give myself totally to you, Jesus. Please help me to stay completely away from anything that could become addictive such as cigarettes, alcohol, drugs, pornography, and (fill in the blank with anything else you can think of).

Guide me, Father. Teach me how to make wise choices. I love you, and I'll trust you with my life. Amen.

Q. *My seven year old brother loves to get me in trouble. I don't know what to do to make him stop. I've told my parents, but they don't do anything about it. How can I make him stop?*

A. This may not be the answer you're wanting, but here goes. You probably *can't* make him stop. None of us can control other people's behavior. But here's the good news: This is an important lesson for you to learn. Why? Because we go through our entire lives having to deal with people who don't behave right, and the sooner we learn to handle it, the better.

Even though he's saying stuff to get you in trouble, promise God that you'll always be honest. People often get accused of something that wasn't their fault, and there's no defense. It's not fair, but it happens. God knows your heart, and he can help you endure the consequences of your brother's behavior—even though you're not to blame. Jesus was crucified on a cross, and he was completely innocent. He has the power to help you in similar situations.

There will probably be others in your life who will blame you for something you didn't do, or tell lies about you. Keep being honest. Eventually, those around you will see you as a young lady of integrity and great character. And the dishonesty in others will be seen as well.

One more thing: Even though you may get in trouble when you don't deserve it . . . you can still feel really good about yourself by knowing you're an honest girl. Always tell the truth.

Softcover 0-310-70045-0

Pick up a copy today at your local bookstore!

Own the entire collection of Lily fiction books by Nancy Rue!

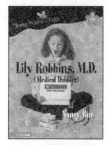

Here's Lily! (Book 1)
Softcover 0-310-23248-1
The Beauty Book companion

Lily Robbins, M.D. (Book 2)
Softcover 0-310-23249-X
The Body Book companion

Lily and the Creep (Book 3)
Softcover 0-310-23252-X
The Buddy Book companion

Lily's Ultimate Party (Book 4)
Softcover 0-310-23253-8
The Best Bash Book companion

Ask Lily (Book 5)
Softcover 0-310-23254-6
The Blurry Rules Book companion

Lily the Rebel (Book 6)
Softcover 0-310-23255-4
The It's MY Life Book companion

Lights, Action, Lily! (Book 7)
Softcover 0-310-70249-6
The Creativity Book companion

Lily Rules! (Book 8)
Softcover 0-310-70250-X
The Uniquely Me Book companion

Available now at your local bookstore!

Zonderkidz™

With this wonderful collection of non-fiction companion books, author Nancy Rue tackles everyday girl stuff from a biblical perspective!

The Beauty Book ...
It's a God Thing!
Softcover 0-310-70014-0
Here's Lily! companion

The Body Book ...
It's a God Thing!
Softcover 0-310-70015-9
Lily Robbins, M.D. companion

The Buddy Book ...
It's a God Thing!
Softcover 0-310-70064-7
Lily and the Creep companion

The Best Bash Book ...
It's a God Thing!
Softcover 0-310-70065-5
Lily's Ultimate Party companion

The Blurry Rules Book ...
It's a God Thing!
Softcover 0-310-70152-X
Ask Lily companion

The It's MY Life Book ...
It's a God Thing!
Softcover 0-310-70153-8
Lily the Rebel companion

The Creativity Book ...
It's a God Thing!
Softcover 0-310-70247-X
Lights, Action, Lily! companion

The Uniquely Me Book ...
It's a God Thing!
Softcover 0-310-70248-8
Lily Rules! companion

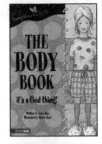

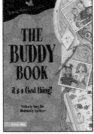

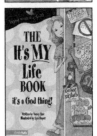

Available now at your local bookstore!

Zonderkidz™

NIV Young Women of Faith Bible
GENERAL EDITOR SUSIE SHELLENBERGER

Designed just for girls ages 8-12, the *NIV Young Women of Faith Bible* not only has a trendy, cool look, it's packed with fun to read in-text features that spark interest, provide insight, highlight key foundational portions of Scripture, and more. Discover how to apply God's word to your everyday life with the *NIV Young Women of Faith Bible*.

Hardcover 0-310-91394-2
Softcover 0-310-70278-X
Slate Leather–Look™ 0-310-70485-5
Periwinkle Leather–Look™ 0-310-70486-3

NEW!
NEW!

Available now at your local bookstore!

Zonder**kidz**™

More great books from the Young Women of Faith™ Library!

Dear Diary
A Girl's Book of Devotions
Written by Susie Shellenberger
Softcover 0-310-70016-7

Girlz Want to Know
Answers to Real-Life Questions
Written by Susie Shellenberger
Softcover 0-310-70045-0

Take It from Me
Straight Talk about Life from a
Teen Who's Been There
Softcover 0-310-70316-6

YWOF Journal: Hey! This Is Me
Written by Connie Neal
Wire-O 0-310-70162-7

Available now at your local bookstore!

Zonder**kidz**™

Coming August 2002

Rough & Rugged Lily (Book 9)
Softcover 0-310-70260-7
The Year 'Round Holiday Book companion

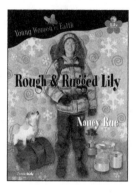

Lily Speaks! (Book 10)
Softcover 0-310-70262-3
The Values & Virtues Book companion

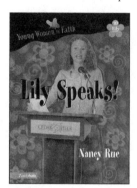

The Year 'Round Holiday Book ... It's a God Thing!
Softcover 0-310-70256-9
Rough & Rugged Lily companion

The Values & Virtues Book ... It's a God Thing!
Softcover 0-310-70257-7
Lily Speaks! companion

Zonder**kidz**.

We want to hear from you. Please send your comments about this book to us in care of the address below. Thank you.

Zonder**kidz**™

Grand Rapids, MI 49530
www.zonderkidz.com